The Old Man and the Bear

The Old Man and the Bear

By Wolfram Hänel

Pictures by Jean-Pierre Corderoc'h

**Translated by
Rosemary Lanning**

North-South Books

NEW YORK

First published in the United States, Great Britain, Canada,
Australia, and New Zealand in 1994 by North-South Books,
an imprint of Nord-Süd Verlag AG, Gossau Zürich, Switzerland.

Copyright © 1993 by Nord-Süd Verlag AG, Gossau Zürich, Switzerland
First published in Switzerland under the title *Der kleine Mann und der Bär*
English translation copyright © 1994 by North-South Books Inc.

Distributed in the United States by North-South Books Inc., New York.

Library of Congress Cataloging-in-Publication Data is available.
ISBN 1-55858-253-3 (TRADE BINDING)
ISBN 1-55858-254-1 (LIBRARY BINDING)

A CIP catalogue record for this book is available
from The British Library.

1 3 5 7 9 10 8 6 4 2
Printed in Belgium

Far away in the north runs a great,
wide river. Every spring, salmon swim up
that river from the sea, their silver backs
flashing as they leap out of the water.

In the old days there were so many salmon that they hardly had room to swim.

Back then an old man called Mahony
used to come down to his log cabin by
the river every spring.

He would fling open the creaky
wooden shutters, sweep the floor, brush
away the cobwebs, and scour the rust
from his frying pan. Then he'd take out
his fishing rod, pull on his rubber boots,
and wade out into the river.

Then a brown bear came to live in the forest on the other side of the river. He was known as Big Bill, and big he certainly was. When he stood up on his hind legs, he was taller than a man.

In spring, as soon as the snow melted, Bill ambled down to the river and out onto some flat rocks. This seemed to him an excellent place to fish.

But then he looked up and saw
the old man. They were both startled,
but neither of them wanted to move.
The fishing was too good right there.

So they just turned their backs to each other and went on fishing—the old man with his rod, and the bear with his huge paws.

But Old Mahony wasn't too happy
about fishing alongside a bear. He turned
around and yelled, "Scram!"

Big Bill stared at him in silence
for a minute.

Then he opened his mouth wide in a
ferocious growl, turned away, and went
on fishing.

Old Mahony was just about to shout
"Scram!" again when he felt a sharp tug
on his fishing line.

Old Mahony had hooked a fine, plump
salmon. He waded quickly back to the
shore and lit a fire to cook the fish.
He was a happy man as he watched the
juicy fish sizzling over his campfire.
After his meal he sat for some time on
the riverbank, patting his full stomach
contentedly.

As he sat there, Old Mahony saw the bear walking back into the forest, holding a fish between his teeth.

The bear had had a good
day's fishing too, and was
feeling just as happy and well
fed as the old man.

Things went on in the same way for some time.

The old man and the bear met at the river each morning. Old Mahony always yelled "Scram!" and the bear just growled back.

Then they would both start to fish,
each in his own way. There were more
than enough salmon for both of them.
And if nothing had changed, they would
both have been perfectly happy.

But then, one morning, Big Bill
decided to move a little way downstream.
There the fish would pass him first and
he could scoop them all up before they
reached Old Mahony.

"That's not fair!" growled the old man.

But the river
was too deep for
him to stand
opposite the bear.

That day old Mahony had to go
without any fish for his supper.
He sat by his fire, grumbling and
spooning plain white beans out of a tin.
He was not at all happy now.

Big Bill, on the other hand, was well
fed when he disappeared into the forest
as usual.

Old Mahony was not going to let
the bear defeat him. The next morning
he dragged an old net out of his shed
and sat in the sun, sewing and knotting,
until he had mended all the holes.

Big Bill stood by the river and watched him suspiciously, but he couldn't figure out what the old man was doing.
So he went on fishing. He caught a lot of salmon and ate them with gusto, smacking his lips noisily to annoy Old Mahony.

That evening Old Mahony had to eat
beans for supper again. But this time
he didn't grumble. When he went to
bed, he was smiling happily and
rubbing his hands.

Early the next morning Old Mahony walked briskly along the river, looking very pleased with himself. He was going downriver, the way the salmon came.

Round a bend in the river
Old Mahony came to a place where
rocks reached out from both banks. He
stretched his net from one rock to
another. No salmon could swim upriver
now. He walked back to watch Big Bill
waiting in vain for salmon.

"Now scat!" bellowed Old Mahony across the river.

Big Bill was so startled that he forgot to growl back.

Old Mahony shouted, "Tonight *you'll* be eating beans! Ha ha!"

The bear was furious.

He pulled himself up to his full height.
He wasn't going to let a little old man
tell him what to do! But then he slipped
and fell back into the river. The current
caught him and he went spinning across
the water toward Old Mahony.

There was no time for Old Mahony to jump out of the way. He was swept off his feet and whirled down the river, along with the bear.

In a swirl of arms and legs the old man and the bear were swept round the bend straight into Old Mahony's net. There was a loud ripping noise as the net tore and silvery fish leapt out in all directions.

The old man and the bear gasped for
air and swallowed water. Still the river
swept them along, until at last they
landed on a little island. They crawled
out onto the sandy beach and lay there,
coughing and spluttering.

Old Mahony was still coughing when
Big Bill lifted his nose and sniffed. Then
Old Mahony smelled something too. It
was honey! Delicious, sweet, sticky honey
from wild bees! Big Bill snuffled and
growled. He had spotted the bees' nest
close by, in a hollow tree.

The bear reached into the hollow tree,
and when he pulled his paw out, it was
covered in honey.

Just then the bees came back!

First one, then four, then more and more. They swarmed round Big Bill, buzzing furiously.

The bear waved his paws to shoo them away. But the bees were all around him. They settled behind his ears and under his chin. One even stung him on the nose. Big Bill howled with pain.

"Run for it!" shouted Old Mahony. "Dive into the river!"

Big Bill ran as fast as he could, plunged into the water, and disappeared under the surface. The angry bees buzzed straight ahead and were soon gone.

The big bear was gasping and coughing when he came back up for air. Old Mahony mopped his brow and grinned. Big Bill grinned too. He ambled back to the honey tree, took another pawful of honey and offered it to the old man. Old Mahony smacked his lips as he licked the sweet honey from the bear's paw.

"We should work together, you and I," he said. And the bear agreed.

That night they built a campfire
together and drew up a menu for the rest
of the summer.

For breakfast they would have fresh salmon. They would skip lunch, and for supper there would be tinned beans, with honey for dessert.

"Even salmon is boring if that's *all* you have to eat," said Old Mahony with a chuckle.

About the Author

Wolfram Hänel has lived for most of his life in Hannover, Germany. He studied German and English literature and has worked as a photographer, a graphic artist, a copy writer, a teacher, and a playwright. Today Wolfram Hänel writes children's books, plays, and travel guides. He has a wife and a daughter, and would like to live by the sea, or better yet, on an island. There is a little one named Inishturk that would be perfect. It has eighty-four inhabitants, four fishing boats, no cars, and only one telephone . . . .

About the Artist

Jean-Pierre Corderoc'h was born in Nantes, France, and studied art at the Ecole des Arts Décoratifs in Strasbourg. He lives with his wife, the illustrator Eve Tharlet, and their son Kilius in a two-hundred-year-old converted farmhouse in Brittany.